Beast Quest®

FERROK
THE IRON SOLDIER

With special thanks to Michael Ford

To Freddie James Mills

www.beastquest.co.uk

ORCHARD BOOKS
Carmelite House
50 Victoria Embankment
London EC4Y 0DZ

A Paperback Original
First published in Great Britain in 2012

Beast Quest is a registered trademark of Beast Quest Limited
Series created by Beast Quest Limited, London

A CIP catalogue record for this book is available from
the British Library.

ISBN 978 1 40831 847 8

5 7 9 10 8 6 4

Printed in Great Britain by CPI Group (UK) Ltd, Croydon, CR0 4YY

The paper and board used in this paperback are natural recyclable
products made from wood grown in sustainable forests. The
manufacturing processes conform to the environmental regulations of
the country of origin.

Orchard Books
An Imprint of Hachette Children's Group
Part of The Watts Publishing Group Limited
An Hachette UK Company
www.hachette.co.uk

FerroK
THE IRON SOLDIER

BY ADAM BLADE

ORCHARD

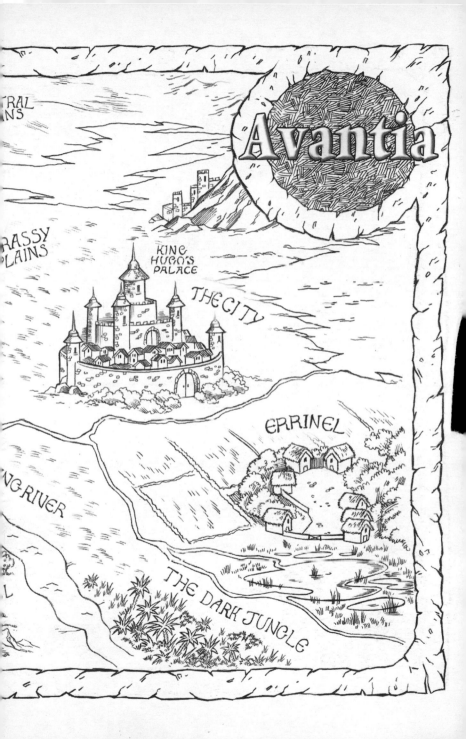

STORY ONE

Greetings, Avantians,

You think you're so safe, don't you? You believe that Tom and the King's soldiers can protect the kingdom from any threat.

Well, you're wrong. I've been watching Captain Harkman and his cadets. All he teaches them is to polish their boots and march in time. He doesn't realise what great warriors those boys and girls could be, with the right leader! Fortunately, I know just who can lead them – a Beast!

I'm sick of living in the shadows. Tom thinks he's invincible with the Golden Armour in his possession, but who's to say a witch can't wear it? The Armour will be mine!

To war!
Petra the Witch

CHAPTER ONE

A NEW NIGHTMARE

Tom's eyes snapped open. *Fire!*
The bedroom was filled with black
smoke. Flames licked through the
broken windows. He threw off the
covers and heard Storm's panicked
whinnying outside. *The stables must
be ablaze too!* Tom pulled his tunic
over his mouth and crawled across
the bare floorboards, coughing in the

smoke. As he reached out to seize the door handle, the door shook from the other side, splintering down the middle. Tom backed away. *Where are my sword and shield?* The door thundered again and was smashed off its hinges. Tom stared as a huge hand reached into the room – a hand made of boiling fire. The fingers, molten-red, grasped at him. There was no escape. His life was over...

Tom sat up with a gasp. His eyes adjusted slowly to the darkness of the room. There was no fire, no smoke. The door was intact and through the windows he could see the pale light of Avantia's moon bathing the stables. Elenna lay on a mattress on the floor, with Silver curled up beside her. She was spending a night in Errinel, breaking up her journey to visit her Uncle Leo.

"Just a nightmare," Tom muttered, as the sweat cooled on his skin.

I've been fighting Beasts for too long, he thought. *Now I'm fighting them in my sleep as well!*

He swung his legs out of bed, careful not to disturb Elenna. Padding across to the window, he realised there was an orange glow from across the stable yard – the fire in his Uncle Henry's forge.

It was still the middle of the night. *A strange time to be at work,* Tom thought.

"What's the matter?" asked Elenna sleepily.

Tom turned to see her leaning on one elbow, rubbing her eyes.

"Uncle Henry's working."

"Now?" asked Elenna.

Tom nodded. "It seems strange. I'm going to investigate."

Elenna scrambled up. "Not without me, you're not."

Silver shifted, lifting his head. His eyes opened lazily, then he settled his chin back down on his front paws.

"I guess Silver's going to stay put," Tom said, smiling.

As they crept across the yard, the ting-tang of hammer blows carried through the air. At the open forge doors, Tom saw Uncle Henry silhouetted against the fire. He lifted his arm and brought it down again on the anvil, showering sparks around his feet. As he worked, beads of sweat dripped from his head onto the molten metal.

Tom knocked on the door as he entered. "What are you making at this hour?" he asked.

Uncle Henry half-turned, his eyes wide in alarm. "Oh, it's you," he said, relaxing. "You'll see in a moment."

He plunged the metal into a trough, using tongs. With a hiss, a great cloud of steam rose from the water. When he drew the tongs back out, they gripped the steel blade of a sword.

"Who needs a weapon made at night?" asked Elenna.

Someone cleared his throat. Tom spun around. There, in the shadows of the forge, stood a man with a helmet under his arm.

"Captain Harkman!" Tom said.

The commander of King Hugo's soldiers stepped forwards. "Greetings Tom and Elenna," he said. He took the blade from Uncle Henry with a nod of thanks and began to

wrap twine around the hilt. "I've
been leading a group of cadets on
a survival training mission," he
continued. "We met a pack of hyenas
crossing the Winding River."

"Was anyone hurt?" asked Tom.

"I'm pleased to say not," said
Captain Harkman. "The cadets formed

a ring, as they've been trained to do, to protect themselves. We beat off the pack, but I lost my sword in the river."

Tom looked to Elenna, who was frowning. Something didn't add up here. Why would Captain Harkman need to get a new sword made, when there were hundreds in the Castle armoury?

Captain Harkman's eyes darted to Uncle Henry.

He's hiding something, Tom thought.

"Well," said Uncle Henry, wiping his hands. "I'm going back to my bed. Leave payment on the anvil."

Captain Harkman waited for him to leave, then shut the door. "Truth is," he said in a low voice, "the survival training has been called off. Aduro contacted me and asked me to fetch you both."

"Us?" said Tom. "Is there some threat to the kingdom?"

Captain Harkman nodded. "Aduro has sensed evil within our borders. He couldn't be sure where, but he wants us to be on our guard."

"So that's why you came here," said Tom. "We need to get to the palace at once."

Elenna rushed to the door. "I'll saddle Storm," she called back.

Captain Harkman reached inside his jerkin and pulled out a scroll. "Aduro asked me to give you this," he said.

Tom took the scroll, broke the red wax seal and unfurled it. The paper was blank.

"I don't understand..." he began.

A blue mist rose off the parchment, gathering into a column like swirling dust. Slowly, the shape of a miniature figure appeared, hovering just a finger's breath above the paper.

"Aduro!" said Tom.

"Ah!" said the Wizard. "Well done Captain Harkman for delivering this message. Tom, I couldn't leave the Palace myself. Avantia needs your help."

"I'll do anything you need me to," said Tom, feeling a rush of pride.

"Good," said Aduro. "Go with Captain Harkman and his troop of cadets. I have soldiers patrolling the south, east and west of the kingdom. I want you to check the north, because I sense the evil is concentrated there. If you come across any trouble, get word to me."

"What sort of trouble?" Tom asked.

Aduro bobbed over the parchment. "Portals," he said. "Watch the sky for them. I sense our enemy is at hand."

"Malvel?" Tom asked.

Aduro shook his head gravely. "Not this time," said the Wizard. "A new foe. Be careful, Tom."

His image faded away, leaving the parchment blank once more. Tom rolled it up and handed it to the

Captain. "Whatever evil has come to Avantia," he said, "we won't rest until it's vanquished!"

CHAPTER TWO

EMERGENCY PATROL

Elenna appeared in the doorway, leading Storm by the reins. She had her quiver hooked over her shoulders. Silver stood close by, his eyes bright and ears pricked.

"If we ride fast and hard," she said, "we can reach the Palace by mid-morning."

"There's been a change of plan," said Tom. "Aduro's sent word we're to patrol the north with Captain Harkman and his cadets."

"Where are they?" asked Elenna.

"Follow me," said Captain Harkman.

They walked across the yard to the end of the stable block. Under the moonlit orchard, Tom saw a group of two dozen boys sleeping amongst the trees. Horses, one for each pair of cadets, munched quietly at the grass.

"They're not much of a fighting band yet," said Captain Harkman, "but they've got plenty of spirit."

A light breeze blew through the orchard, and an apple dropped off one of the trees. It bounced off a brown-haired boy's head.

"Ouch!" he said, sitting up quickly.

Elenna giggled and Tom couldn't stop a smile spreading over his lips.

"They're more quick-witted
than they look," muttered Captain

Harkman. "Samuel! Show some respect to your new comrades."

The boy's eyes widened as he took in Tom and his companions. He leapt to his feet and gave a clumsy salute. "Yes, sir!"

"They look like a fine force," said Tom. "Tell them to be ready at once."

Captain Harkman leant close to Tom's ear and said, "Samuel's father is King Hugo's Master of Arms. He's only been with us for ten days. Couldn't win a swordfight against a scarecrow, to be honest with you."

Tom grinned and left Captain Harkman and Elenna to gather the cadet troop. He ran back to his chamber to retrieve his sword and shield. He wondered what could possibly await them in the north. Would this ragged band of boys be of help?

As he left again, a faint pink light crept over the eastern horizon. His Aunt Maria came bustling from her parlour door, cheeks flushed. Her hands were covered in flour and she clutched a small sack.

"Now, Tom," she said, "if I'd known you and Elenna were going to be rushing off, I'd have baked you one of my special pies. Here's some bread and cuttings from the roast." She threw her arms around him.

Tom felt the breath being squeezed out of him. Over his aunt's shoulder he saw Uncle Henry in the doorway behind. The old man lifted a hand and smiled.

Will I ever see them again? Tom wondered, as he pulled himself free and walked over to his horse.

They rode out of Errinel bathed in pale morning light. Tom and Elenna galloped at the head of the column with Captain Harkman leading his cadets behind on their horses.

"I can't get used to having so many people with us," said Elenna. "Normally it's just you and I on a Quest."

"It's a big responsiblity, for them," Tom said. "I hope Aduro knows what he's doing."

Tom kept his eyes on the sky, looking for tears or odd coloured clouds – the tell-tale signs of portals opening from other worlds. But for now, the sky was clear blue.

It was late morning when they reached the foothills of the Northern Mountains, and they rested beside a stream so the horses could drink. The cadets looked tired and grimy, apart from Samuel, who trotted up beside Storm.

"That's an impressive shield," he said to Tom.

Tom pulled the shield onto his arm. The six tokens from the Good Beasts of Avantia gleamed in its surface, but he didn't want this boy to know their true power. "Just something I picked up on my travels," Tom replied.

"No one believes that!" said Samuel. "People say—"

Captain Harkman nudged his horse closer. "Leave Tom alone," he said.

"He's no bother," said Tom.

"Back in line, all of you," called the Captain. "And keep your eyes sharp."

They fell into a column as they climbed a rocky mountain path.

Tom began to wonder if Aduro was wrong. Perhaps it was a false alarm, and there was nothing living in these mountains but wild cats, snakes and eagles. The Good Beast Arcta would be lurking somewhere, but Tom didn't sense any warning from the feather in his shield.

The sun had reached its highest point and Captain Harkman had gone to the rear of the line when Samuel rode up alongside Tom again at the head of a windy pass. Tom saw a grin twitch on Elenna's lips.

"What age were you when you had your first sword?" asked the cadet.

"A real one?" said Tom.

"Of course," said Samuel. "I was twelve."

"I was too," said Tom. "But there's more to being a soldier than having a sword. You have to be able to use it."

Samuel patted the sword hanging from his belt. "Captain Harkman told me I was the most promising swordsman in the troop."

"Then you should be proud and keep practising," said Tom.

Samuel fell quiet, but not for long. "People say you're the greatest warrior the kingdom has ever known," he said.

Tom blushed. "You shouldn't believe everything you hear," he said, though he couldn't help feeling proud. He'd fought many Beast Quests – more than most Avantians would ever know about.

"My friend William says your father Taladon was better though," Samuel added.

Tom winced as fresh pain cut through him. His father hadn't been dead long. He had been killed by one of the cursed Knights of Forton. He'd lain in the snowy plains, his blood leaking from him to stain the white flakes. There was nothing Tom could have done. *So why do I feel so useless?*

"Tell us, Samuel," said Elenna quickly, "what else has Captain Harkman taught you?"

Samuel, riding just ahead, looked back over his shoulder. "Well, we learned how to—" A low rumble cut off his words.

"What was that?" muttered Elenna.

The cadet's horse scrambled to one side as the path suddenly opened up below its hooves. Tom heaved Storm sideways as the crack widened. He couldn't do a thing as Samuel lurched out of his saddle with a cry. "Help me!" he called, before disappearing

into the black abyss.

It all happened so quickly, and there was nothing Tom could do but watch.

CHAPTER THREE

AN ANCIENT MINE

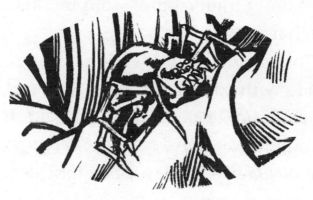

"Stop!" Elenna called to the others. "There's been an accident!"

Tom jumped out of the saddle and scrambled to the edge of the opening. Pebbles broke away from the torn ground, rattling out of sight, and leaves floated into the gloom.

"Samuel!" he called.

No answer.

Tom called again, and heard only

his voice echoing in the darkness. *How deep is it?* he wondered. *Could Samuel possibly have survived?*

"I don't understand," said Elenna. "What is this place?"

Tom stared up at his friend, her eyes wide with concern. *I should have told Captain Harkman that we'd go alone*, he thought. *Now this boy's life's in danger. He should never have been on the Quest.*

Captain Harkman rushed towards them. "Is he...dead?" he asked, his face lined with worry.

"We don't know," said Tom. He spotted something glinting in the wall of the crevasse. "A ladder!" he cried, pointing. "This isn't just a landslip — it's man-made."

Elenna peered in as Tom walked carefully towards the ladder. "It must be an old mine," she said.

Tom reached the top of the rusted
ladder. Holding the rungs at the top,
he placed a foot carefully on the
first tread. As soon as he shifted his
weight, the ladder groaned and his leg
broke through the rung. The gathered
cadets gasped and Tom tightened his
grip to stop himself falling. "We can't

climb down this way," he said, pulling himself back out.

Captain Harkman waved back the other trainee soldiers. "Watch for attackers!"

The cadets turned their horses to fan out and drew their swords. Silver began to dig at the loose earth with his paws.

"He's found something," Elenna said.

Tom followed his friend to where the wolf stood. Sure enough, beneath his snout was a collapsed stone slab, partly covered with grime. Tom brushed the dirt away. Letters had been carved into the stone.

"Colton Mines," Tom read. "I've heard of them."

"Me too," said Elenna. "My uncle used to talk about ancient mines in the Northern Mountains. They'd been used to make armour for evil armies, but were lost to Avantia hundreds of years ago."

We must be standing over one of the old mines now! Tom thought.

"I heard different stories," said Captain Harkman. "When I was a boy, old men in my village used to talk of a village called Colton. A hero came from there, they said, and he fought monsters."

Tom glanced at Elenna.

Monsters? Tom thought, as the hairs stood up on his neck. *Or Beasts?*

"Perhaps Aduro was wrong to ask us to check the skies," Tom said, careful to ensure that only Captain Harkman and Elenna could hear. "Maybe the threat we face has been lurking below our feet."

A faint groan drifted up from the depths.

"Samuel!" said Captain Harkman. "He's still alive!"

"We need ropes," said Tom. "Do you have some?"

Captain Harkman turned to the pale-faced cadets. "Finn, Liam and Theo!" he yelled. "Collect all our ropes and tie them together. Quickly!"

The three cadets sheathed their swords, jumped from their horses and passed between the others, gathering a rope from each. They quickly knotted the ropes into a chain that would stretch as tall as King Hugo's castle walls.

"I'll need your cadets to hold the end while I go down," said Tom.

"I'm coming too," said Elenna.

Tom smiled grimly at his friend. "Thank you," he said. "But I'll go first and make sure it's safe."

As the three cadets gripped the rope a few paces back from the edge, Tom looped the other end around his waist. He braced his feet against the lip of the crack.

"Good luck," said one of the cadets, and the other two nodded

encouragement with thin smiles.

"You'll need this," said Captain Harkman, thrusting a lighted candle into his hand. "Be careful."

Tom lowered himself over the edge. The rope dug into his skin. Down here, the air was musty and cold. Tom tried to brace his feet against the dripping walls. Here and there he saw beams of rotten wood that would have once held the mine-shafts up. Rocks were marked with the rough-hewn scars of pick-axes and other tunnelling equipment.

Suddenly, his feet slipped off the wall and he dropped quickly until the rope tightened around his middle. It creaked as the cadets above struggled to hold him. At least, with Arcta's eagle feather in his shield, Tom didn't have to fear falling to his death.

"Are you all right?" Elenna shouted down.

Tom called back. "I'm fine. Keep lowering me!" Then he heard a rustling all around. *Bats?* he wondered. The scurrying sound came again. "Samuel!" he called.

His only answer was a quiet moan.

As he jerked lower, his feet lost purchase on the wall and he spun helplessly on the rope. The candle threw its light in a wild circle, illuminating the dripping black walls on every side. Something soft brushed his arms, then fell like silk over his face. Tom shook his head and saw long, sticky white strands coating his clothes.

Spider's webs!

Two pinpricks of red light shone on the wall ahead of him. Then two more sparked into life beside them. And another pair. To Tom's horror, the wall seethed as hundreds of spiders turned their eyes upon him. Each was as big as his fist, with hairy legs and pulsing bodies.

One of the wriggling creatures crouched, tensing its legs. Then it leapt off the wall, landing on Tom's waist. He fought down the scream in his throat. Another spider jumped and landed with a soft thump on his leg. Others followed, and Tom felt them crawling up his back as he hung helplessly clutching the candle. Spiders crept their way over his arms and legs, scattering beneath his clothes. The cadets were still lowering him.

I must be near the bottom now...
Pain shot through his shoulder as

one of the spiders sank its fangs into
his skin. Tom grimaced and shook
himself, trying to throw the spider

off. He felt legs dancing up the skin of his neck. If these creatures were poisonous he might not have long left. Another stabbing pain pierced his wrist, and the muscles of Tom's hand went into a spasm so that he let go of the candle. It fell down, down, down, its light vanishing in a wink.

"Are you all right Tom?" Elenna

called, her voice muted. He couldn't
see a thing.

As the spider climbed his face,
Tom clenched his mouth closed. He
was alone in the pitch black with
creatures crawling all over him –
and Samuel was nowhere in sight.

CHAPTER FOUR

UNDERGROUND MENACE

Tom willed his pounding heart to slow down and used his free hand to bat the spider from his face. Shrouded in darkness, he brushed as many of the others off as he could. He'd lost count of how many times he'd been bitten – he could only hope that the spiders' poison wouldn't affect him too much. His thrashing feet found the ground, and he unlooped the rope from his waist.

In the gloom, lit only from the crack of light above, he saw the spiders scurrying off to safety. Pain throbbed all across his body. "I'm down!" he called up, unsure if they'd hear him at all.

"Help me..." mumbled a weak voice. Tom looked around and saw a pale glimmer. Samuel was lying on the ground, using his sword blade to reflect what light trickled down. As Tom walked towards him, picking his steps carefully over the rough ground, he noticed something odd. There were footprints, evenly spaced, in the dirt.

Surely Samuel didn't walk down here, he thought. *Not once he'd fallen all this way...*

Tom crouched beside the cadet.

Blood trickled down the side of
Samuel's face from a cut across his
temple. His tunic collar was already
soaked.

"Lie still!" Tom said. "We'll get you
out of here soon."

Samuel grimaced. "It's my ankle,"
he said. "I think it's broken."

Tom felt gingerly along Samuel's
leg and saw through the meagre

light that the boy's foot was bent at a strange angle. "Don't move," said Tom. He tugged the green jewel from his belt and remembered how he'd won it defeating Skor the Winged Stallion.

"What are you doing?" Samuel asked.

"You'll see," said Tom.

He held the jewel over the broken ankle, feeling warmth spread through his fingers. Samuel gasped as his foot rotated. In hardly any time at all he was stretching out his leg and rolling his foot from side to side. "It's mended!" he said. "That's amazing."

"Let's just keep it between us, though," said Tom, slotting the emerald back into place. "Can you stand?"

Samuel nodded. Tom helped the

young cadet to his feet. Tom's eyes picked up something further along the passage beyond Samuel. His mouth went dry. It was a skeleton, propped up against the wall, the flesh long rotted away from the pale bones. Protruding from the ribs was an arrow shaft.

What happened down here? Tom wondered. *There must have been a fight of some sort.*

None of this felt right. The sooner he got Samuel to safety the better.

Then I can face whatever else is down here...

Samuel was still hobbling slightly, but they reached the dangling rope. Tom quickly looped it over the cadet's head and under his armpits, and made sure the knots were secure. "Use your feet against the wall to keep you steady," he said, "and hold the rope with both hands."

Samuel nodded. "Thank you!" he said. "I didn't know if I'd ever get out again."

Tom cupped his mouth with his hands and called up. "Samuel's coming up! Heave!"

The rope tightened, creaked, and slowly lifted Samuel off the ground. His face was white with fear.

"Are you coming next?" whispered the cadet.

"Soon," said Tom. "I'm just going to have a look round first."

Tom watched him slowly hoisted upwards. He glanced around again. *Time to find our enemy.* The skeleton seemed to watch him from empty eyesockets.

A sudden purple light burst over

him. He heard a cry of panic and saw Samuel plummet down once more. He just had time to rush forward and catch the boy. They landed in a tangle of limbs.

Tom eased himself out from beneath Samuel. "Are you all right?" he asked.

Samuel put a hand to his bleeding head. "I think so." But his face was paler than ever and his eyes brimmed with tears.

Elenna's voice called down: "What happened?"

Tom didn't know how to answer. His hand followed the line of rope tied to Samuel and found the end, singed and frayed. *Something, or someone, doesn't want us to escape*, he thought. Tom drew his sword and turned to face the darkness. "Who's there?" he called.

Another purple flash blinded him. Tom crouched over Samuel to protect him as the pebbles and earth rained down. When it finished, Tom stood up.

He crept forwards into the darkness, shield ready on his arm and sword brandished. The passage followed a

slight bend, past the skeleton. Tom
sensed a person breathing, waiting,
just out of sight.

"Tom?" shouted Elenna. "I'm
coming down."

"No!" Tom yelled back. "We're
all right! Just send another light."

He didn't want his friend coming
below. Not until he'd found out what
they were facing.

Samuel whimpered in fear behind
him. "Don't go down there," he
hissed.

Tom squinted into the darkness and
saw the arch of a doorway off to one
side. "Come out, coward," he said.
"I know you're there."

Mocking laughter drifted from the
shadows and a shape slinked away
like a shred of night.

CHAPTER FIVE

MAN OF IRON

A light above made Tom glance up. "Just what we need," he said.

Captain Harkman and Elenna had tied a lantern to a rope and were lowering it down. Tom shrugged his shield onto his back, caught the swinging lantern and untied it. "I'll be back," he said to Samuel, who nodded silently, his eyes wide.

Tom strode down the passage. Silver

veins of metal gleamed in the walls,
waiting to be mined. He found more
footprints leading to a doorway, but at
the threshold he paused, holding the
lantern up ahead of him. The door
was metal, ringed with iron studs.
The frame was lined with dozens of
skulls. *This is no ordinary mine*, Tom
thought, shuddering. *Perhaps Captain's
Harkman's stories are true...*

Tom turned his sword in his hand,

and smashed the hilt against the rust-streaked door. Clanging echoes boomed through the cavern.

"Come out!" he called.

He stepped back as the heavy door creaked open. The light from his lamp pooled in a circle on the ground. At first it was only blackness beyond, but Tom saw the shadows move as a huge body bent over to stoop through the door. Its limbs were black, and Tom made out a shape like a man's, but three times as tall. The shadow unfolded and towered above him.

"What are you?" Tom asked.

The Beast didn't speak. He clutched a sword as long as Tom, its blade glinting in the gloom. Two green jewels sparkled in the hilt, and the Beast pointed the tip towards the lantern in Tom's hand. The small

door that shielded the oil flame
swung open of its own accord.
The flame streaked through the air
towards the Beast. *He's sucking up the
fire!* Tom thought.

A flash of orange blinded him and
he heard a bang. Tom was thrown
backwards and slammed into the wall
of the passage with a cry of pain. It
was like he'd been kicked by a horse.

As the orange glow seeped away, Tom gasped. The Beast stood before him still, but now flames licked and swarmed over his body like a huge bonfire. The sword had mysteriously vanished. Tom made out plates of dented bronze armour held together by rivets the size of his fist. Tendrils of smoke curled off the Beast's limbs, but he didn't seem to feel any pain.

He's alive with flame! Tom marvelled.

A horned helmet encased the Beast's head, and slits revealed eyes glowing red as embers plucked from the forge. Two horns emerged from each side of the helmet like a bison's, and another curled upwards from the Beast's forehead. Black teeth like broken shards of coal grinned at him with hatred. Around his waist the Beast wore a belt of thick bronze,

and a plaque at the front was gouged
with letters.

"Ferrok!" Tom read aloud.

The Beast lowered one of his hands

and laid it across the plaque. His other hand swirled in the air, the fingertips glowing red. The Beast launched a net of fire through the air. Tom didn't have time to lift his shield as the fiery ropes fell over him. He cried out and shook the net off, but already pain seemed to scorch his insides. He felt his bones grow hot and his blood boil in his veins. Tom staggered backwards, staring in horror at his hands as the skin began to blister. He wanted to cry out, but his breath lodged in his parched throat and all that emerged was a wail.

Tom fell to his knees, and crawled back across the ground towards Samuel. But how could he protect the boy, when he could barely stand?

The pain had eased by the time he reached the cadet, whose eyes widened in horror.

"What happened to you?" he asked. "I heard…"

Samuel's voice trailed off and Tom turned to see Ferrok lumbering along the passage behind him. Flames surged over his body and Tom felt the baking heat on his face. The cadet began to scramble backwards and Tom struggled to bring his shield around. If he could use Ferno's scale, he might save them from the worst of the flames.

"Tom!" called Captain Harkman. "Tom! What's going on down there?"

Ferrok's armoured head jerked upwards at the sound. Placing one hand on his belt again, he drew the other back.

He gets his power from the belt, Tom realised. *He's going to launch more fire.*

"Get back!" he cried out, but his voice was lost in a fit of coughing.

The Beast's arm jerked upwards and a ball of flame left his hand. Like a miniature sun, it shot towards the entrance of the shaft. Shouts of horror from the cadets pierced the cavern and sparks showered down

over Tom and the injured boy. Tom
had always been in awe of Epos's
fireballs, but here was another Beast
with the same power. *Perhaps even
greater*, he thought.

Ferrok bellowed with laughter as
he cast more fireballs towards the
surface, illuminating the upper parts

of the collapsed mine. Tom heard screams and wails from the cadets. As Ferrok hurled his deadly missiles, the flames around him grew in strength.

Tom struggled to his feet, and drew his sword.

"I can help too," said Samuel. As the boy's hand moved towards his own weapon, Tom remembered Captain Harkman's description of the cadet's sword skills back in Errinel.

"No," he said. "Leave this to me."

The Beast was still gazing up the tunnel to the mine entrance. As Tom approached the iron giant's back, the heat became unbearable. His hand slipped on the hilt of his sword, and he felt his hair crisp at the ends. Despair swept over him. *How can I defeat this Beast if I can't even get close to him?* he wondered.

Sweat pricked Tom's body, soaking his clothes. In the passage walls, through narrowed eyes, he saw the glittering trails of iron soften and seep through cracks, dripping fat drops to the ground. The seams of metal melted and pooled.

Ferrok stamped in the puddles of liquid metal as he continued his assault on the cadets on the surface. But instead of burning him, the droplets of melted ore seemed to meld into his armour, hardening over his body.

Then Tom understood. Ferrok was a Beast made of molten iron!

CHAPTER SIX

FERROK'S CURSE

The silver threads poured off the walls and snaked across the ground.

"I'm coming!" shouted Samuel. Tom spun around and saw the cadet, sword brandished, as he leapt between the puddles of super-heated metal.

"Stay back!" called Tom.

Ferrok turned from the entrance to the shaft and his red eyes settled on

Samuel. The Beast's laughter sounded through the cavern. "You cannot escape my iron bonds!" he boomed.

He threw out a hand, and great lashings of molten iron poured from his fingertips, spreading across the ground, snaking towards Samuel. The cadet hopped from foot to foot, trying to avoid the bubbling metal.

"Leave him alone!" shouted Tom. "Fight me!"

Then Samuel tripped. He threw out a hand to steady himself. His fingers touched a river of flowing iron. Samuel's scream split the air and the cadet lurched backwards, rolling over in agony and clutching his injured hand to his chest. Smoke reached Tom's nostrils.

Ferrok was still busy hurling fireballs, so Tom ran to Samuel's side. He was sitting against the passage wall, cradling his hand. The skin had been scorched away, leaving a claw of red and blackened flesh. But as Tom got closer he saw the grimace slip from the young soldier's face. A smile replaced it. Samuel lifted his hand in front of him. Tom jerked away, open-mouthed at what he saw.

A sheen of silver spread over the red-raw and blistered skin. Before Tom's eyes, Samuel's hand was covered in a shining gauntlet of iron, but it wasn't like any armour Tom had ever seen. Samuel flexed his fingers as easily as if the gauntlet weighed nothing at all. On his chest, Tom made out an engraved emblem of Ferrok's horned head.

"Sam?" Tom said, unsure whether

or not to move nearer.

The cadet leapt to his feet, and his eyes wore a mad, hateful look. All his fear had gone.

"He's mine now!" bellowed the Beast.

The cadet drew his sword in a rapid movement and Tom only had a moment to bring round his shield. The blade smashed into the wood, almost throwing him off his feet.

"Samuel, it's me – Tom!" he cried.

The young boy laughed pitilessly. "I know who you are," he sneered, his voice rasping and low. "And it'll take more than that scrap of wood to protect you."

Tom couldn't believe what he was hearing. "Samuel, listen to me. Ferrok has enchanted you, but remember who you are – a cadet of King Hugo's army, and loyal to the good forces of Avantia."

Samuel swished his sword in rapid slashes.

So much for his lack of sword skills, thought Tom.

"I'm loyal only to the Iron Soldier," Samuel growled.

As Tom watched in horrid fascination, the metal gleaming over Samuel's hand began to spread over his wrist and up his forearm. The cadet's body trembled as it seeped past his elbow and shoulder. The smile on his face became a wide grin as the molten iron covered his chest and torso, then climbed up his neck to encase his head. In no time at all, his whole body was covered in armour that shone in the dark passage.

"Ready to play?" Samuel mocked.
Tom drew his sword, steadied his
shield on his arm, and dropped into
a fighting stance. He knew he could
never bring himself to hurt the boy,
but he couldn't let himself be injured
either. As Samuel circled him, he had
no doubt this was a fight for his life.
I have to keep Samuel at bay until we find

a way to undo this evil magic, he thought.

A rumble from the other end of the passage made Tom glance away. Ferrok was trying to pull away some of the rocks. With hands like huge flaming shovels, he attacked the walls, tearing down rocks around his feet. Debris scattered over his shoulders, but he didn't seem to care.

If he keeps doing that, thought Tom, *we'll all be buried alive. Perhaps that's what he wants. We have to get out of this place!*

Samuel leapt over a smoking puddle of iron and brought his sword down in a vertical swipe. Tom dodged sideways and rammed the boy with his shield. The wood gave a dull clang as it met the strange armour.

"You'll have to try better than that," said Tom.

Samuel stabbed, and Tom parried then smacked the flat side of his blade against Samuel's helmet. The blow would have sent any normal soldier reeling, but Samuel merely shook his head. "You're supposed to be the best swordsman in the kingdom, aren't you?" he said. "If that's the best you can do, Avantia's in trouble."

Anger surged through Tom's

chest. With a cry, he feinted towards Samuel's head, then kicked out. His boot caught the cadet's stomach, but it was like kicking a stone wall.

"Maybe Elenna will give me a better fight," said Samuel. "I'll enjoy killing her."

Tom stepped forwards with a series of lunges to Samuel's legs. He dodged or blocked each one and sparks flew from their clashing blades. The cavern shook violently as boulders crashed down from Ferrok's assault on the walls.

"No wonder your mother left you," jeered Samuel. "She was probably ashamed to have such a pathetic son."

Anger swelled through Tom's veins. As Samuel lunged at him, he ducked under the blade and drove his own sword home, straight through the boy's midriff. It sank through a chink in Samuel's armour up to the hilt. The cadet's eyes widened in horror.

"No..." Tom muttered. *What have I done?*

He withdrew his blade, expecting Samuel to sink to his knees. But the cadet remained standing. Tom saw there was no blood on the blade, and the hole in Samuel's armour magically sealed.

"That's impossible!" said Tom.

Samuel arched an eyebrow. "You've made Ferrok angry now."

Tom dived to one side as a fireball seared towards him. It smashed into the ground right where he'd been standing. Tom saw the walls of the shaft had been smashed up completely by Ferrok, caving in to

make a steep slope of broken stone
towards the surface.

"Kill him now, Master!" shouted
Samuel.

Ferrok tipped back his head in
a mighty laugh that shook loose
more stones. He dropped one hand
to the plaque of his belt, and in the

other a fireball grew. Beyond him, through eyes streaming with smoke, Tom saw the distant faces of Elenna and Captain Harkman watching helplessly from above. Samuel, his sword brandished, blocked Tom's path deeper into the mines, and more molten iron poured off the walls.

Tom could see there was no way out. *I'm going to burn to death!*

CHAPTER SEVEN

SILVER IN DANGER

As Ferrok hurled his fireball, Tom
called on the power of Ferno's scale
to magically protect him from fire,
and hoisted up his shield. Flames
exploded all around him, but the
shield held. He blinked and coughed
in the choking smoke and saw
Samuel striding towards him, his
sword pointed at Tom's head.

"No!" screamed Elenna. Over the

slope of collapsed rubble something grey streaked down towards them. Ferrok turned to look as Silver darted between the Beast's legs. Silver leapt up, catching Samuel with his front paws and sending the evil cadet sprawling on the ground.

"Good boy!" Tom cried.

With a growl, Ferrok marched towards them both, flames trailing from his fist. Before Tom could stop him, Silver leapt at the Iron Soldier, only to be batted away with a flaming foot.

The brave wolf rolled across the ground, whining as fire singed his fur. The Beast raised a massive foot and tried to stamp on him, but Silver scampered away, deeper into the cavern. At the edge of the darkness, he turned and growled at Ferrok.

He's trying to lure the Beast away, Tom realised.

"After the creature!" shouted Ferrok, bounding in pursuit. Samuel ran in his master's footsteps, through the archway where Ferrok had first appeared. Soon they were nothing but a faint glow disappearing further underground.

I hope Silver can outrun them, Tom thought. *I need to get above ground to warn the others.*

Tom picked his way over the collapsed mine walls. He didn't need a rope and climbed back to the mouth of the shaft over the slope of loose rocks until at last he hauled himself into daylight. Elenna held out a hand to heave him to safety.

"Are you all right?" she asked.

Tom looked down at his singed and soot-stained clothes. "I can fight on," he said.

"What was that thing?" she said.

"It's the Beast Aduro sensed," said Tom. He quickly explained how he'd encountered the Iron Soldier and the fate which had befallen Samuel.

Captain Harkman ran a hand through his hair. "It's my fault," he muttered. "I should have told Aduro this mission was too dangerous for untrained soldiers."

The rest of the cadets were still standing well back down the path, some thirty paces away, holding their horses by their reins.

Tom put a hand on the captain's shoulder. "Don't worry – we'll rescue Samuel."

"What about Silver?" Elenna said, her face creasing with worry. "He hates fire. If Ferrok corners him down there..."

A roar shook the ground, and then they heard a yelp. Silver flew through the air ten feet high, landed and slid across the earth. He hobbled upright and limped to Elenna's side, his body trembling.

"Oh, Silver!" she gasped.

Tom saw burn scars along his flank and his ear was torn and bleeding. He felt a twist of guilt in his stomach. *He suffered for me.*

Elenna crouched to comfort her companion. Tears pricked her eyes as the injured wolf licked her hand. "It's all right," she said. "We'll help you get better."

Tom glanced into the opening, but he couldn't see Ferrok or Samuel. Then the ground shook beneath his feet, and he heard wild shouts of "What?" and "Help!", and horses neighing.

"Over there!" said Captain Harkman.

He was pointing towards his cadets. Their horses reared and bucked, then scattered as the ground broke open. Half the cadets were stumbling, clinging to one another, and the other half had already lost their footing. Something like a tree root burst forth from the stony soil between them. But the roots flexed and clenched.

That's not a tree, Tom realised. *It's a hand!*

Ferrok's fist clamped onto the ground and the Beast's head rose from the earth. Flames writhed over his armoured limbs and the cadets froze with terror at the monster climbing out of the ancient mine. "What is that thing?" one cried.

"Run!" Tom shouted.

Ferrok stood over the cadets and flicked his wrist. Gobbets of fire and molten iron scattered over the young soldiers, making them scream. Samuel clambered out beside the Beast, laughing. "Meet my new

friend Ferrok!" he called.

Slowly the cadets' smouldering
bodies became still. A pall of smoke
rose around them.

"Are they...dead?" gasped Captain Harkman.

Tom tried to unsheathe his sword, but a hand caught his arm. Elenna shook her head. "Look!" she said.

Through the smoke, shadows lurched upright. One by one the cadets were standing, but they no longer wore the uniform of Avantian soldiers in training. Each was covered in the same casing that covered Samuel.

Tom saw the emblem of the Beast's horned head engraved on their chests as they lined up beside Ferrok. *They're his slaves now*, Tom realised.

Ferrok loomed over his minions and turned southwards. His cadets turned too. Through the slits of his helmet, the Iron Soldier's red eyes narrowed.

"What's he looking at?" mumbled

Captain Harkman.

Tom concentrated, calling on the power of the Golden Helmet. He made out the tips of distant towers on the horizon. "King Hugo's palace," he said.

Ferrok opened his mouth, and a jet of flame spurted out. "To war with the King!" he shouted.

Tom had to think fast. There was no way he and his two companions could face down both the Beast and his army. "Captain," he said. "Take Storm and head back to the city. Warn them what's coming."

"But what about you two?" said Captain Harkman.

"We'll do what we can to hold back the enemy," said Tom. "Now go – quickly."

Captain Harkman's face was creased

in a frown, but he backed away towards where Storm waited beside a boulder.

"Tom...we've got company," said Elenna. His friend had already strung an arrow to her bow.

Tom saw some of the iron-clad cadets marching forwards with Ferrok behind them. Samuel led the others.

"You tried to leave me down there to die!" he spat.

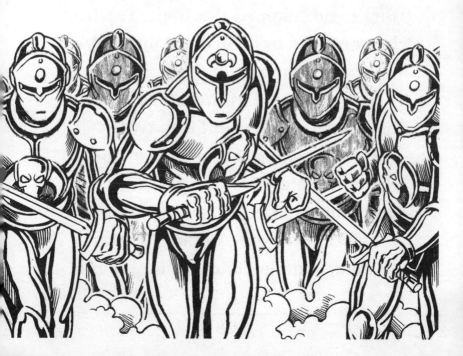

"Tom tried to rescue you!" Elenna shouted back. "Now stop there, or else." Her fingers twitched on her bowstring.

Samuel grinned. "March on, my comrades. Her weapons are harmless."

Elenna loosed the arrow. Quicker than Tom's eyes could follow, Samuel seemed to jerk to one side and raise an arm. He caught the arrow mid-flight and snapped the shaft. The iron head melted in his palm, joining the rest of his armour.

Elenna gasped in horror. The enchanted cadets split into two columns, one pacing to either side. Silver, despite his injuries, bared his teeth and snarled.

The cadets closed behind Tom and Elenna, completely encircling them.

They marched in perfect time. Dozens of eyes glinted with hatred behind their visors.

Ferrok raised an arm, and another net of fire dangled from his fingers. Tom faced the Beast and refused to look away. "Avantia will fight you, even if we're gone," he said.

Ferrok glared down and smiled in triumph, but it was Samuel who spoke. "The people of Avantia will face a choice," he said. "Join us, or be burned to cinders at our feet. Which would you prefer?"

Tom looked towards Elenna and she shook her head grimly.

"We'll never fight for an Evil Beast," he said.

"I thought you might say that," said Samuel. "Brave, but stupid."

I hope Captain Harkman makes it back

in time, Tom thought, *because our Quest is about to end.*

There was the sound of something hissing through the air. Ferrok had flung the deadly net of fire towards them...

STORY TWO

My plans are coming together nicely. Our two friends are about to meet their deaths – how delightful! Then the army will march on the palace and I will be one step closer to wearing the Golden Armour. I can almost feel its power now. I will be invincible!

This is what I brought Ferrok back to life for, to defeat King Hugo and to take over his kingdom. Ferrok has been waiting hundreds of years to be released. The least I can do is give him a good battle to enjoy. Keep reading, if you dare to face the outcome. You're about to watch the good people of Avantia be squashed beneath my feet.

In anticipation,

Petra the Witch

CHAPTER ONE

HELP FROM THE SKIES

Tom grabbed Elenna to yank her out of the way. He heard a sizzling sound and Elenna screamed in pain, clutching her leg. The edge of the net had burned part of her clothes away, leaving red flesh beneath.

The cadets jeered.

"That's just a taste of the pain that awaits you," said Samuel.

Tom supported Elenna as the pain in her face turned to anger. "You won't get away with this!" she shouted.

Ferrok lifted another net of flame over his head. He bellowed with laughter, and ash cascaded from his shaking shoulders. It made Tom think: *Perhaps we can fight fire with fire...* He reached for the Dragon's

Scale embedded in his shield. Since he'd won it from Ferno on his first Quest, Tom knew he could call on the Good Beast in times of peril. And what better Beast to battle Ferrok than a Fire Dragon?

"Hear me, Ferno," he whispered. "We need you now."

"We'll crush this petty kingdom beneath our metal fists!" Ferrok cried.

"Not while there's blood in my veins, you won't," said Tom.

Ferrok turned to him. The red glow of the Beast's stare almost burned his skin. "There won't be blood in your veins for much longer," he hissed. "Soon they will flow with boiling iron!"

Samuel chuckled. "It's time we added two more soldiers to our ranks, I think."

Tom understood when he saw Ferrok's fingers dripping with molten iron. Just a few drops would be enough to imprison him and Elenna in metal shells. The soldiers stepped aside as Ferrok stamped closer to use his magic.

SCREECH!

Everyone glanced up. The vision in the skies made Tom's heart soar. The massive leathery wings of Ferno burst through the clouds. The Beast's scaly head, which looked carved from jagged black rock, swung around to face the Iron Soldier, and his eyes narrowed.

Placing a hand on his belt, a fireball blossomed in Ferrok's palm. He flung it skywards at the approaching Dragon, but Ferno tipped sideways to dodge. The fireball crashed into

the mountainside, burning a patch
of bushes to cinders. Ferno swooped
towards the Evil Beast, talons first,
with a screech that made the hairs
on Tom's neck stand on end.

As the Fire Dragon plunged down,
the cadets scattered in terror, letting
Tom and Elenna slip from their trap
with Silver.

Ferno slammed into Ferrok,

flattening the Iron Soldier. They fought on the ground, with flames licking over them. Tom knew Ferno's scales protected him from flame, and Ferrok seemed to thrive in fire. It was an even match. Ferno attacked with his deadly talons and tearing jaws, while Ferrok pounded at the Good Beast and tried to pin his wings.

"Go on, Ferno!" Elenna shouted.

"Kill the pathetic Beast!" Samuel cried.

All the cadets were watching the battle between the Beasts, and Tom saw he had a chance. *If I can get close, I might be able to help the Fire Dragon...*

He crept forwards, and drew his sword slowly. Ferno had Ferrok on his back, thrashing as he snapped with his jaws. Ferrok tossed his horned helmet back and forth like

an enraged bull, trying to slash
Ferno's flesh with the cruel tips. One
of the Evil Beast's arms lay across the
ground, and Tom lifted his sword.
If he could injure the Iron Soldier,
it might tip the balance further in
Ferno's favour.

"Stop him!" shouted Samuel.

Tom jerked his head to the left just
in time to see two cadets rushing
at him. They smashed into his side
and threw him to the ground. Tom
struggled, but they held him fast.
Beyond he saw that Elenna was being
held by two more. She writhed in
their grasp, but it was useless.

From his position pressed against
the ground, Tom saw the Fire Dragon
rake his claws across Ferrok's face.
Molten iron hissed and sizzled from
the wounds like blood. Tom thought

Ferno was getting the upper hand until he saw the Evil Beast reaching for his belt. *He's going to try some magic,* Tom realised. "Ferno, be careful!" he called.

As soon as the Iron Soldier touched the plaque, the flames dancing over his limbs turned hard and sharp, becoming hundreds of bristling iron points like the teeth of a saw.

Ferno keened, pushing off as the jagged points pierced his scales. Blood seeped from scratches and cuts across his body as he struggled to hover. Through Nargar's jewel in his belt, Tom sensed the Beast's pain.

Ferrok tipped back his head and laughed. The spikes on his body became flames once more, then died to nothing. The Iron Soldier crouched close to the ground. "Climb on, cadets!" he ordered.

Ferno was still flapping wildly, trying to stay aloft as the young soldiers scrambled up Ferrok's legs and onto his arms and shoulders. Their iron armour didn't seem to slow them down at all. The ones holding Tom sprang away from him, joining

their comrades. Others clambered
up onto his back and the rest clung
to the plates of his armour. Ferrok
stood slowly, with a sound of grinding
metal and pointed south towards the
horizon. Tom made out the distant
plume of dust from Storm's pounding
hooves.

"To the palace," Samuel bellowed.

"And to victory!"

With a huge leap, Ferrok jumped over their heads. When he landed the ground shook, and he ran on, bounding down through the foothills towards the Plains. Each stride was thirty paces at least, faster than any galloping horse. Elenna gripped Tom's shoulder.

"Captain Harkman and Storm!" she said. "They won't make it in time!"

CHAPTER TWO

WARNING THE PALACE

"We have to go after them," said Elenna.

As the words left her mouth, Ferno sagged to the ground. Silver limped towards the Dragon.

"First we have to tend to their wounds," said Tom, loosening Epos's talon from his shield. "We can't fight a Beast like Ferrok in this state."

It didn't take long to heal the

cuts and burns both creatures had suffered, but every moment that passed Tom imagined the Beast getting closer to the city. Soon Silver was lively as ever, running around in impatient circles. Ferno lowered his body against the ground for them to climb on his back.

"Thanks, old friend," said Tom, gripping the ridge of a scale to pull himself up. "This is the quickest way back to the palace."

"Wait!" said Elenna. "Silver's found something."

The wolf was running back from the boulder with a rolled up piece of parchment in his mouth. He dropped it at Elenna's feet.

"It's the scroll Captain Harkman was carrying," said Elenna. "He must have dropped it."

As she unfurled the paper, Aduro's image bobbed up. His face was grave. "I sense danger, Captain. What... Captain? Tom, Elenna, where is Captain Harkman?"

Tom glanced at Elenna. He couldn't bring himself to say the truth – that if Ferrok had caught them, the Captain and Storm were likely dead already. Tom felt a lump form in his throat as he thought of his proud stallion.

"We're not sure," Elenna said. "But it doesn't look good. The Captain was riding to warn you, but he's being chased by a Beast."

"From a portal?" asked Aduro.

"From underground," said Tom. "A giant made from molten iron called Ferrok. He's turned all the cadets into his soldier-slaves and they're marching towards the palace."

"Ferrok, you say," said Aduro, his brow creasing. "This is bad. Worse than I could have imagined. I thought Avantia was rid of the Iron Soldier."

"You knew about him?" asked Tom.

Aduro nodded. "My predecessors wrote of him in their books," he said, "but he was supposed to be trapped deep in the Skull Cell, in the old armouries near Colton."

"What does he want?" asked Tom. "Why attack the city?"

"Ferrok always does another's bidding," said the Wizard. "I can tell you more face to face." He said, glancing nervously about. "In these dangerous times, I don't trust messages sent by visions. You must come back at once."

"We'll ride with Ferno," Tom said. "We'll be back at the palace by sunset."

"There's no need for that," Aduro replied. He raised a hand and clicked his fingers. Silver whined uneasily. Slowly the mountains, the sky, and Ferno blurred.

"Farewell, old friend," Tom called to the Dragon.

Ferno blasted a spurt of fire from his jaws, then everything vanished.

Tom felt weightless for a moment, floating in a purple light, then there was hard ground beneath his feet once more. Aduro stood before him in the flesh. They were at the edge of the palace courtyard, standing on the cobbles beside the stable block.

"Still no sign of our enemy!" called a voice.

Tom glanced up to where King Hugo stood on the battlements, wearing his silver armour. Only now did Tom become aware of all the soldiers rushing about, carrying weapons. Archers lined the walls, peering out, and the drawbridge was creaking up.

"We're not taking any chances," said Aduro. "Ferrok is an ancient Beast, but if the legends have any truth, he's one of the most deadly. They say he has a magical belt which makes iron."

"And fire," said Tom. "He can turn normal people into his slaves."

"But you said he's being controlled by another," said Elenna. "And if it isn't Malvel, who's behind this new evil?"

"I'm not sure," said Aduro.

Someone with a talent for resurrecting dead Beasts, thought Tom.

He was about to say the name of an old enemy, when he heard her usual giggle. Tom spun around and saw the Master of Arms pushing a girl in front of him. Greasy hair hung over her face and she wore a tattered green robe.

"I found this young sorceress in the armoury!" said the Master of Arms.

"Petra!" said Tom. "I might have known you were involved!"

CHAPTER THREE

THE WITCH'S CURSE

Petra pushed a lock of hair out of her eyes. "How lovely to see you again, Tom," she said. "And your little helper, Elenna."

King Hugo ran down from the battlements. "What's she doing here?" he asked.

"I found her in the Armoury," said the Master of Arms. "She'd blown the lock from the door with a spell."

"Well, throw her in the dungeon, where she belongs," said the King. "We'll deal with her when the current threat has passed."

"Wait," said Tom. "What did you want in the Armoury, Petra?"

"She was trying on the golden gauntlets," said the Master at Arms.

Petra gave a lopsided smile. "Just because Malvel's not around anymore, doesn't mean the rest of us can't have some fun."

Tom stepped close to Petra, lowering his voice. "Only the Master of the Beasts can wear the Golden Armour," he hissed.

"Ha!" she said. "It's not for me, stupid!"

The Master of Arms looked at Tom, then at Aduro. "I heard the cadets had got into some bother," he said. "I hope my boy's not been causing trouble."

"No trouble at all," Tom said quickly. "He's a brave fighter, that's for sure."

"That he is," said the Armourer. "He's the pride of my life, that boy."

Tom felt guilty, but he didn't want to alarm the Master of Arms. *I'll find a way to rescue Samuel, if it's the last thing I do*, he thought.

As Petra was dragged away to the dungeons, she shot a hateful glare towards Tom and Elenna. "Where's Storm, by the way?" she called.

Tom's blood boiled, but he restrained himself. *I have to think clearly.* "We need to man the defences," he said. "Ferrok and his army cannot be allowed to breach the walls."

King Hugo's face was pale. "We sent half of the soldiers out on patrol to other parts of the kingdom," he said. "They won't be back in time."

Tom drew his sword. "Then we have to fight twice as hard."

A horn sounded across the courtyard, and a soldier shouted down from the walls. "I see something..." His face was pale as ashes. "Something huge."

Tom ran up the steps quickly and scanned the horizon between the battlements. He saw the dark shape of Ferrok, running unwearied across the fields towards the castle.

"I must go and prepare my magic," said Aduro. "I fear this battle will test us all."

He clicked his fingers and vanished.

"All soldiers to the walls!" Tom

shouted. "Everyone else inside!"

The armed men and women of
the city stood in even lines at the
walls, joined here and there by brave
citizens carrying makeshift weapons,
like scythes and threshers. An old
cobbler clutched a pair of leather
shears, and one of the kitchen staff
brandished a bread paddle from the

bakers' ovens. Tom's heart surged
with pride.

*We'll need all the help we can get
to defeat Petra's Beast*, he thought.

"Ready the catapults!" roared King
Hugo. "Let's show this Beast what
we're made of."

Ferrok stopped when he was a
hundred paces from the city walls,
and the cadets clambered down from
his body, forming a line either side of
the Iron Soldier. There was no sign
of Storm or Captain Harkman, and
Tom couldn't bring himself to think of
their fate. Flames burst out once more
over the Beast's body, lighting up the
sky.

Tom heard the creaking of the
catapults being drawn back, as
soldiers wound the mechanisms. They
worked on platforms just below the

walls and the ropes strained as they loaded rocks into the wooden bowls.

Tom stared out at Ferrok and his band of armour-clad cadets. *Two catapults won't be enough to stop our enemies*, he thought. *We need a Beast's help too.*

Tom thought about calling Ferno

again, but the Beast had done enough. Tom touched the talon in his shield, and called to the Flame Bird of Stonewin: *Come, Epos!*

There was the sound of hooves and suddenly a shape moved from behind the Beast – a single horse and rider, both coated in the same silvery armour. It took Tom a moment to realise the shape of the stallion was familiar.

"Storm..." he breathed. Which meant the rider had to be Captain Harkman. They'd become Ferrok's victims, too.

Storm let out a ferocious neigh that travelled through the air to Tom.

How could he do this to you? Then Tom hardened his heart, and looked back to see soldiers pouring oil over the rock missiles. Another held a lit torch to each, and the rocks burst into flame

with a *whumph*. Soldiers shouted
down the range of their target and
those operating the catapult moved
them slightly on their wheels.

Tom surveyed the plain. Ferrok
and the cadets hadn't moved, but
the enchanted Storm was stamping
his hooves, eager to attack. He had
no idea that boiling oil was waiting
for him. Could Tom allow his faithful

stallion to enter into battle, with every risk of losing his life? But what choice did he have? He had to defeat Ferrock.

Epos broke through the clouds with an angry screech, a fireball clutched between her talons. Her wings blazed in the sunlight like polished bronze. She circled in the air then, with a screech of fury, she dropped the fireball over the Evil Beast. Gasps rose up from the people on the

battlements – some of them would never have seen a Beast before.

"Fire!" cried King Hugo, following Epos's lead.

Two huge fiery balls arced over the walls like comets. At the last moment, Ferrok held out both hands, catching each of the flaming rocks in his palms as easily as if he were playing catch with apples. Epos's fireball crashed into his chest and he staggered back a single pace. A wall of flame exploded from his body, but when the smoke cleared, Ferrok was still standing proud. He crushed the two missiles into his chest and his body swelled even larger.

Epos swooped away with an anxious caw.

We've just made Ferrok even stronger! Tom thought.

CHAPTER FOUR

ATTACK OF THE IRON ARMY

The Iron Soldier waved his minions on, and half the cadets ran to the walls with unnatural speed.

"It's all right!" called King Hugo. "The battlements of the city cannot be breached."

As they reached the edge of the moat, the cadets stopped. Seemingly from nowhere, their hands sent out

darting ropes of flame. They swung
them up towards the battlements, and
iron grappling hooks appeared at the
end, clanging into place and catching
on the stone. The defending soldiers
backed away.

"That's impossible!" one shouted.

"Evil magic!" cried another.

The iron-clad cadets swung across

the water and began to clamber up the walls. Tom swallowed back his fear, and drew his sword. Suddenly the Palace looked more vulnerable than ever. *If the city falls, there'll be no one to protect the rest of the kingdom!*

"Hold steady!" he called. Elenna was already shooting down arrows, and managed to knock one of the cadets down into the moat. He landed with a cry. Tom used his sword to slice through one of the fiery ropes and another cadet tumbled off the walls. This time there was no splash. Tom looked over the side and saw the cadet clinging grimly to a ledge on the wall. Hand over hand he began to climb, his armour clanging on the stone.

Tom looked up. Captain Harkman was riding beside the remaining cadets behind Ferrok, who had gathered a fireball in his hand. The Beast drew back his arm and hurled the blazing orb towards the closed drawbridge. Tom heard a mighty crash as flames burst into the palace courtyard with splinters of wood. The missile must have severed the winding chains, because the remains of the drawbridge slammed down.

"The castle's breached!" shouted a soldier.

Tom waited for the cadet to reach

the top of the wall, then brought his sword hilt down hard. With a cry, the cadet plunged backwards towards the moat. But Tom couldn't rest. Captain Harkman was spurring Storm into a gallop and broke away from the rest of the group, straight for the drawbridge. He drew a sword from his scabbard, the sword made by Tom's Uncle Henry that very morning. Only now the blade glowed red-hot like a poker left in the fire. Using the power of the golden helmet, Tom could see the expression of hatred twisting the Captain's face.

"Fire at the Captain!" Tom called to Elenna. His friend adjusted her aim and fired. The arrow thudded into Captain Harkman's shoulder, but he only kicked Storm's flanks harder. Ferrok had begun to run towards

the castle too, and his cadets were
swarming up the walls like ants.
Soon they'd reach the top.

"Kill them all!" bellowed Captain
Harkman.

Suddenly a shadow fell over

him. Tom glanced up and saw Epos
swooping down once more. Her
talons clutched another fireball,
and she hurled it at the approaching
Captain. Storm leapt over the
streaking ball of flame, barely
breaking stride and it scorched a
path across the plains. The armoured
horse and rider were almost at the
drawbridge.

The first of the cadets climbed
over the top of the battlements and
began to fight the soldiers guarding
the walls. Tom hardly knew which
to attack first, but his eyes were
still drawn downwards towards the
Captain's deadly charge. The moment
Storm's hooves hit the drawbridge,
Epos swooped low. There was no
fireball this time, and Tom realised
in horror that the Good Beast was

on a collision course.

"No!" Tom cried. It was too late.
Epos thudded into Storm's side,
driving both horse and rider off the
drawbridge. With a panicked whinny
and flailing hooves, Storm and
Captain Harkman plunged into the
moat with a massive splash. Ferrok
sprang back from the curtain of water.

Tom pushed himself away from the walls in horror. Wearing all that armour, both would surely drown. *I've got to help them...*

But as he turned, he saw Samuel launch himself at the King on the catapult platform and wrap his hands around Hugo's throat. The King dropped to his knees as he struggled against Samuel's magical strength. Tom leapt over a flaming rope and pointed his sword at the cadet's throat. "Leave him," he said, "or you die."

Samuel laughed, and from the King's darkening face, Tom guessed he was squeezing harder. He smashed the flat of his blade across the back of Samuel's neck. The blow broke the cadet's grip, but Samuel swung an arm, catching Tom across the jaw.

He toppled back with a cry and saw
Samuel aim a vicious kick at Hugo's
midriff. The King tumbled backwards
down a set of wooden steps into the
courtyard below. Servants rushed to
his side, and Tom was glad to see the
King stand, unsteady but uninjured.

Samuel got to his feet and drew his
sword. "You should join us, Tom," he

said. "That's if you want to be on the winning side."

Tom brandished his own blade. "This isn't over yet," he said.

Samuel grinned. "It will be soon."

CHAPTER FIVE

FERROK'S TRIUMPH

A huge crash of stone sounded below
and the crumpled iron portcullis flew
into the courtyard. Cadets poured in
after it. Silver ran straight at them,
leading a charge of defenders. Tom
saw a woman wielding a rolling pin,
and an old man shaking a walking
staff at the invaders. The ragtag army
fell upon the armoured cadets as
Samuel laughed and lunged. Tom

somersaulted over his enemy's blade and off the platform. He landed in the courtyard below to face the new onslaught. Elenna arrived at his side, her face streaked with soot but her jaw firmly set. Ferrok stood in the entrance tower, surrounded by licking flames. In his hand was the giant sword Tom had seen in the mine. Ferrok was hacking into the walls inside the tower, and the soldiers above clung to each other as the whole structure heaved.

"Get down from there!" Tom called. "It's going to fall!"

In the courtyard, soldiers and cadets did battle. Normally the untrained cadets would have been no match, but now that they wore their enchanted iron armour it was taking three or four soldiers to fight

individual cadets. Swords, shields
and spears clanged as the cadets'
eyes glowed an evil red.

It won't be long before someone's killed, thought Tom.

He thought of Storm, plunging into the moat. Was there any chance he could have survived? As he remembered the awful moment, another memory crept into his mind – Ferrok leaping away to avoid the water. *Why? Unless he was afraid...*

With a crunch of grinding stone, the main gate tower of the palace leant inwards. Soldiers cried out, running for cover as the huge gateway collapsed in a thunder of masonry and clouds of dust. Tom hoped the soldiers had escaped in time.

When the air stilled, Ferrok stood inside the shattered remains, beating his chest. "Fear my fists of iron!" he roared.

A purple shape streaked through

the air towards him.

"Aduro!" Elenna cried.

The Wizard was shooting bolts
of blue light from his palms. They
blasted Ferrok backwards towards
the drawbridge. He lashed out with
swinging arms, as Aduro ducked and
weaved in the air. But Tom could see

the bolts were becoming weaker, and still Ferrok was standing. As Aduro darted forward, the Iron Soldier caught him with the back of his hand and sent Aduro spinning through the air. The Wizard rolled and slid across the cobbles. Tom ran to his side.

"Are you all right?" he asked.

Aduro shook his head, smoke rising from his burned robes. "I thought I could help," he mumbled. "But my magic isn't strong enough."

Tom and Elenna took an arm each and helped drag Aduro to the stable doorway and away from the fighting. Bales of hay were already ablaze, shielding them behind a curtain of flame. Through the swathes of black smoke, Tom saw Ferrok stride into the middle of the courtyard. Molten iron oozed between his teeth like drool and spilled out around his feet. It spread in snaking channels between the cobbles towards the clutches of fighting soldiers. Tom knew exactly what would happen next.

"Everyone – out of the way!" he cried.

A few of the soldiers looked up, but most were too busy fighting. The silvery liquid metal lapped around their feet, and one by one they stared down in terror at the hissing molten iron. Their screams were short-lived,

replaced by horrified silence as the iron spread over their bodies.

"They're unstoppable!" said Aduro.

King Hugo and a group of half a dozen soldiers had escaped and gathered beside Tom, Elenna and the Wizard. So far he didn't think Ferrok or his army had spotted them behind the flaming bales.

"We need to fall back," said the King. "In the open, Ferrok can pick us off at will."

"Good thinking," said Tom. "Head for the throne room."

"What are you going to do?" asked the King.

Tom looked to Elenna. "I have a plan."

As the King and his loyal men helped Aduro into the palace, Elenna spoke up. "We can't take on the whole army on our own!" she said.

"That's not my plan," Tom said. "I'm going to give Ferrok what he wants – the Golden Armour."

Elenna frowned. "But then he'll be more powerful than ever," she protested.

"He won't get a chance to wear it," said Tom. "Do you trust me?"

Elenna's forehead creased even more. "Of course."

"Then go to the dungeon," he said, "and release Petra. If I'm right, she'll lead Ferrok to the armour. That's what the two of them want, isn't it? She knows where it is."

Elenna nodded. "And where will you be?"

Tom smiled grimly. "I'll be waiting for them."

"They'll see us," said Elenna. "But I

know how to distract them for
a while." She gave a shrill whistle.
Silver scampered through the smoke
to their side.

When Tom saw the loyal wolf,
he thought about Storm and all the
stallion's brave sacrifices through
so many Quests.

Elenna cupped the wolf's face in
her hands. "I need you to keep our
enemies busy," she said. "Can you
do that?"

Silver yipped twice and broke away,
throwing himself bravely over the
blazing bales and at Ferrok and his
cadets. Tom heard the soldiers shouting
in panic and Ferrok's angry roars.

"Good luck in the dungeons," he
said.

"Petra might suspect a trap," Elenna
replied.

"Tell her we're releasing her because we're desperate and she's the only one who can stop Ferrok," said Tom. "She's vain enough to believe it."

Elenna ran through a passageway into the palace. As Tom watched the pieces of his plan fall into place, he hoped he hadn't made the biggest mistake of his life.

CHAPTER SIX

THE GOLDEN ARMOUR

Using the power of Tagus's horseshoe in his shield, Tom darted from his hiding place at super speed. He sprinted around the edge of the courtyard and under an archway, then up some steps. The Armoury was against the outer wall of the castle.

And right beside the moat, thought

Tom. *That was the key to his plan. If I can dampen Ferrok's flames, perhaps I can drown his power too.*

The studded Armoury door was still hanging off its hinges from Petra's earlier assault. The Golden Armour rested on its stand, glowing magnificently in the half-light. Tom

trailed his fingers over the smooth surface and thought of his father who had possessed the armour before him. Taladon would never have let anyone take it and Tom didn't plan on letting him down now.

A giggle shook him from his thoughts. "Quick, it's this way!" said Petra's voice, coming from the stairs.

Tom hid behind the armour, his back to the wall. The bricks were two feet thick here, with no windows, but he knew the moat was on the other side.

The chamber began to shake with heavy footsteps and and he heard Ferrok's rasping breaths. Petra appeared in the doorway, rubbing her hands together. Her eyes lit up at the sight of the armour. "I told you it was here!" she said. "And that stupid girl

Elenna thought I'd help her! She'll be my maidservant when all this is over."

Heat flooded the room as Ferrok's huge body appeared behind Petra. With blazing fists, he ripped away the stones from around the doorway, and bent over to let himself into the Armoury. He looked bigger than ever to Tom, his armoured chest heaving under a carpet of fire.

"It's ours!" he bellowed.

Tom stepped from behind it, clutching his sword. "Not yet it isn't," he said.

Petra jerked backwards, but then her face relaxed into a wicked grin. "You can't stop us now," she said. "The whole castle is ours. Your King will bow and kiss my feet by nightfall."

The Beast circled the armour, leaning close to inspect it.

"You'll have to get past me first," said Elenna. Tom saw his friend step through the ruined doorway, an arrow pointed straight at Petra.

Ferrok roared in fury and gathered a fireball in his palm. Seeing that Elenna had nowhere to run, Tom swung his sword across the back of Ferrok's ankle. It rang out against the

Beast's iron core. Ferrok spun around, swinging wildly with his flaming arm. Tom ducked beneath. *Time to finish this*, he thought.

"Come on, you lump of metal!" he shouted. "Show me what you're made of!"

Ferrok lumbered past the Golden Armour towards Tom, who stood with his back to the outer wall. He drew back his fist.

"Crush his puny skull!" screeched Petra.

Ferrok's eyes blazed almost white hot with anger as he punched. Tom waited until the fiery hand was just a fraction from killing him, then dived sideways. He heard the Beast's fist drive into the wall and a whole section of the stone crashed away, leaving a gaping hole. Daylight flooded into the room, and the Iron Soldier wheeled for a moment over the moat below. Then his weight carried him over the edge.

"No!" screamed Petra.

As Ferrok toppled, he bellowed with anger and flung a fireball back into the chamber. It sizzled into the ceiling, showering them all with sparks. The Evil Beast plunged into the water below with a sound like a thousand red-hot swords being submerged in a blacksmith's water trough. The moat bubbled and steamed as he thrashed in the water, his body shrinking as he roared. A single iron fist thrust out from the water in defiance. Tom watched the fingers curl, then droop, then shrivel away.

For a moment, he thought he saw
a statue the size of a normal man,
stiff-limbed and black as coal, but
then it sank out of sight.

Ferrok was no more.

"Argh!" called Elenna. She was
on the ground, knocked over, and
Petra was fleeing down the steps. But
there wasn't time to go after her. Tom
heard a crash. The fire was taking
hold of the armoury and the stand
holding the golden armour collapsed,
scattering the different pieces over
the ground.

Elenna rubbed her head. "She must
have used a spell to get past me," she
said, struggling to stand.

Tom raced to help her up. "I need
to rescue the armour," he said. The
Golden Armour was important to the
safety of the kingdom – without it,

there could be no Master of
the Beasts.

"I'll help you," she mumbled.

They quickly scooped up the
armour as the choking smoke and
ash gathered in the wrecked room.
Tom's skin baked in the intense heat
and he could barely see through
his streaming eyes. But they found
the doorway, and threw themselves
into the corridor. The ceiling of
the Armoury collapsed completely,
flooding the room with rubble.

Tom made his way out into the courtyard. Fires burned all around, but already servants and stewards were emerging from the cellars, and forming lines to the well to fetch buckets of water. King Hugo and Aduro, leaning on his staff, were marshalling them. The entrance gate was completely destroyed, but it could be rebuilt. There was no sign of Storm, or Captain Harkman, and across the courtyard, the iron-armoured bodies of Ferrok's army lay strewn and unmoving. Tom's heart almost stopped. Were they dead?

CHAPTER SEVEN

A FINAL FAREWELL

Tom saw a body he recognised and rushed over, dropping to his knees beside the corpse. *Samuel*.

The cadet's face was pale and his features still. Tom reached out and touched his cheek. "Samuel?"

After a short moment, Samuel's eyelids flickered open. Tom's hand went to the hilt of his sword, just in case. But the silvery armour coating

his body seeped away like breaking mist, leaving the plain tunic of the Avantian cadets.

Shame flooded Samuel's face. "I... I don't know what to say. I never meant to... He made me..."

"It's all right," said Tom. "You couldn't help your actions. The important thing is that you're safe now."

All across the courtyard, Tom heard groans as men, women and cadets woke from their nightmares. Their metal shells vanished too. They rubbed their heads in disbelief and surveyed the awful damage.

King Hugo walked among them. Though his armour was dented and his cloak torn, he stood tall. "Take the injured to the infirmary." He helped the old cobbler to his feet and slapped him on the back. "We have survived this day, thanks to our combined bravery," he declared. "As soon as we have repaired the damage, we'll call a feast to celebrate our rescue from the jaws of peril."

"But the danger is still out there," said Tom. "Petra is still free to cause havoc as she wishes."

Elenna lowered her head. "I let her escape," she said. "I'm sorry, Your Majesty."

King Hugo placed a comforting hand on her shoulder. "Nonsense!" he cried. "Without you we would all be under Ferrok's evil magic now."

"Let me go!" squealed a voice.

All heads turned towards the remains of the gate-tower. Tom heard hoofbeats on timber, and realised at once that he recognised the pattern as clearly as if they were his Uncle Henry's footsteps outside his bedchamber in Errinel.

"Storm!" he said.

"I won't go back there!" cried the girl's voice.

Through the smoke trotted Storm. Captain Harkman, soaking wet, sat on the stallion's back. And across the saddle, her hands trussed behind her back, was Petra. The young witch was writhing and spitting curses.

"Look what I found," said the Captain. He slipped off the saddle, leaving Petra there, and dropped to his knees before the king.

"Your Highness," he said. "I beg your mercy."

"Arise!" said King Hugo. "Your sacrifices for this kingdom are well known. You left Aduro's magic scroll with Tom and Elenna, rather than using the magic for yourself."

Captain Harkman blushed and stood up. Tom gave him a smile and a nod of thanks.

"Now then," said the King, pointing to Petra. "What shall we do with her?"

Two soldiers pulled her down and pushed her towards the King. She staggered and almost fell.

"Do you have anything to say for yourself?" asked the King.

Petra giggled. "There's been a misunderstanding, Your Highness," she said. "I never meant any harm."

"You meant to steal the Golden Armour," said Elenna.

Petra shot her a spiteful glance. "I just wanted to borrow it for a while," she said. "What's wrong with that?"

The gathered crowd murmured angrily until King Hugo raised his hand for silence. "The Armour is *earned*," he said. "You tried to obtain it through trickery and bloodshed. What possessed you to awaken Ferrok?"

"I wanted to scare people," sulked Petra. "I didn't know he could do all those other things."

"Didn't know," said Tom, "or didn't care?"

Petra lunged at him, but the soldiers pulled her back. "You think you're so clever, don't you?" she spat. "Why shouldn't I be Mistress of the Beasts?"

"Because you have no honour," said Aduro, stepping close to her. "You spent too long with Malvel as your guide. You've proved time and again that you cannot be trusted and you are an enemy to innocent people. It's up to the King to decide your fate."

The crowd turned to King Hugo. "I'm not a vengeful man," he said, "but the kingdom must have justice. Our prisons are not strong enough to contain your evil, so you must be banished from Avantia forever." He nodded to Aduro.

The wizard pointed his staff at Petra and the tip began to glow scarlet.

"No," said Petra. "I can change, I promise. I like it here. If you'll just let me..."

A bolt of purple light enveloped Petra and cut off her words. She pounded the purple wall with her fists. Aduro muttered a few words Tom didn't understand, then the purple orb shrank to a dot in less

time than it took to blink. The dot
vanished.

"Where has she gone?" asked Tom.

Aduro looked grave, and weakened
by the magic. "Somewhere she will
never return from," he whispered.
"Perhaps one day I will tell you, but
for now..." He cast his hand around.

"For now, we must rebuild."

The crowd scattered and began to lift the broken rocks onto carts and into barrows. Others started to erect scaffolding to hold up walls that might topple at any moment. Tom walked over to Storm, and stroked his nose. "I thought I'd lost you, boy," he said.

The stallion snorted and nuzzled Tom's shoulder.

Elenna wandered over to his side, with Silver close to her legs, tongue lolling.

"Do you think Aduro's right?" she asked. "Have we seen the last of Petra?"

Tom shrugged. They'd defeated Ferrok, but it had taken every ounce of their strength to complete the Quest. How many other Beasts

lay hidden in Avantia, ready to be
reawakened?

"People are always greedy for
power, and jealous of what they don't
have," he said. "If it's not just Petra's
evil we have to face – there'll be
others. But if we stick together, we'll
always be a match for our enemies."

Elenna grinned. "I couldn't agree
more!" she said.

The two of them went to help
an old man lift a piece of broken
masonry. As he straightened up,
Tom gazed out of the open city gates
towards the Avantian horizon.

We're waiting for you, he thought,
sending out a message to unseen
enemies. *Whilst there's blood in my
veins, this kingdom will be safe.*

JOIN TOM ON HIS NEXT BEAST QUEST SOON!

Fight the Beasts,
Fear the Magic

Do you want to know more
about BEAST QUEST?
Then join our Quest Club!

Visit
www.beastquest.co.uk/club
and sign up today!

All books priced at £4.99.
Special bumper editions priced at £5.99.

Orchard Books are available from all good bookshops, or can be ordered from our website: www.orchardbooks.co.uk, or telephone 01235 827702, or fax 01235 8227703.

Beast Quest®

Series 11: THE NEW AGE
COLLECT THEM ALL!

A new land, a deadly enemy and six new Beasts await Tom on his next adventure!

ELKO
LORD OF THE SEA

978 1 40831 841 6

TARROK
THE BLOOD SPIKE

978 1 40831 842 3

BRUTUS
THE HOUND OF HORROR

978 1 40831 843 0

FLAYMAR
THE SCORCHED BLAZE

978 1 40831 844 7

SERPIO
THE SLITHERING SHADOW

978 1 40831 845 4

TAURON
THE POUNDING FURY

978 1 40831 846 1

Series 14: THE CURSED DRAGON
COLLECT THEM ALL!

Tom must face four terrifying Beasts as he
searches for the ingredients for a potion to
rescue the Cursed Dragon.

978 1 40832 920 7

978 1 40832 921 4

978 1 40832 922 1

978 1 40832 923 8

Join Tom on his Beast Quests
and take part in a terrifying adventure
where YOU call the shots!

Win an exclusive
Beast Quest T-shirt and goody bag!

Tom has battled many fearsome Beasts and we want to know
which one is your favourite! Send us a drawing or painting of
your favourite Beast and tell us in 30 words why you think
it's the best.

Each month we will select **three** winners to receive
a Beast Quest T-shirt and goody bag!

Send your entry on a postcard to
BEAST QUEST COMPETITION
Orchard Books, 338 Euston Road, London NW1 3BH.

Australian readers should email:
childrens.books@hachette.com.au

New Zealand readers should write to:
Beast Quest Competition, PO Box 3255, Shortland St,
Auckland 1140, NZ or email: childrensbooks@hachette.co.nz

**Don't forget to include your name and address.
Only one entry per child.**

Good luck!

Read on for an exclusive extract of
CEPHALOX THE CYBERSQUID!

The Merryn's Touch

The water was up to Max's knees and still rising. Soon it would reach his waist. Then his chest. Then his face.

I'm going to die down here, he thought.

He hammered on the dome with all his strength, but the plexiglass held firm.

Then he saw something pale looming through the dark water outside the submersible. A long, silvery spike. It must be the squid-creature, with one of its weird robotic attachments. Any second now it would smash the glass and finish him off...

There was a crash. The sub rocked. The silver spike thrust through the broken plexiglass. More water surged in. Then the spike withdrew and the water poured in faster. Max forced his way against the torrent to the opening. If he could just squeeze through the gap...

The pressure pushed him back. He took one last deep breath, and then the water was

over his head.

He clamped his mouth shut. He struggled forwards, feeling the pressure in his lungs build.

Something gripped his arms, but it wasn't the squid's tentacle – it was a pair of hands, pulling him through the hole. The broken plexiglass scraped his sides – and then he was through.

The monster was nowhere to be seen. In the dim underwater light, he made out the face of his rescuer. It was the Merryn girl, and next to her was a large silver swordfish.

She smiled at him.

Max couldn't smile back. He'd been saved from a metal coffin, only to swap it for a watery one. The pressure of the ocean squeezed him on every side. His lungs felt as though they were bursting.

He thrashed his limbs, rising upwards.

—————

He looked to where he thought the surface was, but saw nothing, only endless water. His cheeks puffed with the effort to hold in air. He let some of it out slowly, but it only made him want to breathe in more.

He knew he had no chance. He was too deep, he'd never make it to the surface. Soon he'd no longer be able to hold his breath. The water would swirl into his lungs and he'd die here, at the bottom of the sea. *Just like my mother*, he thought.

The Merryn girl rose up beside him, reached out and put her hands on his neck. Warmth seemed to flow from her fingers. Then the warmth turned to pain. What was happening? It got worse and worse, until he felt as if his throat was being ripped open. Was she trying to kill him?

He struggled in panic, trying to push her off. His mouth opened and water rushed in.

That was it. He was going to die.

Then he realised something – the water was cool and sweet. He sucked it down into his lungs. Nothing had ever tasted so good.

He was breathing underwater!

He put his hands to his neck and found two soft, gill-like openings where the Merryn

girl had touched him. His eyes widened in astonishment.

The girl smiled.

There was something else strange. Max found he could see more clearly. The water seemed lighter and thinner. He made out the shapes of underwater plants, rock formations and shoals of fish in the distance, which had been invisible before. And he didn't feel as if the ocean was crushing him any more.

Is this what it's like to be a Merryn? he wondered.

"I'm Lia," said the girl. "And this is Spike." She patted the swordfish on the back and it nuzzled against her.

"Hi, I'm Max." He clapped his hand to his mouth in shock. He was speaking the same strange language of sighs and whistles he'd heard the girl use when he first met her –

but now it made sense, as if he was born to speak it.

"What have you done to me?"

"Saved your life," said Lia. "You're welcome, by the way."

"Oh – don't think I'm not grateful – I am. But – you've turned me into a Merryn?"

The girl laughed. "Not exactly – but I've given you some Merryn powers. You can breath underwater, speak our language, and your senses are much stronger. Come on – we need to get away from here. The Cybersquid may come back."

In one graceful movement she slipped onto Spike's back. Max clambered on behind her.

"Hold tight," Lia said. "Spike – let's go!"

Max put his arms around the Merryn's waist. He was jerked backwards as the swordfish shot off through the water, but he managed to hold on.

———

They raced above underwater forests of gently waving fronds, and hills and valleys of rock. Max saw giant crabs scuttling over the seabed. Undersea creatures loomed up – jellyfish, an octopus, a school of dolphins – but Spike nimbly swerved round them.

"Where are we going?" Max asked.

"You'll see," Lia said over her shoulder.

"I need to find my dad," Max said. The crazy things that had happened in the last few moments had driven his father from his mind. Now it all came flooding back. Was his dad gone for good? "We have to do something! That monster's got my dad – and my dogbot too!"

"It's not the squid who wants your father. It's the Professor who's *controlling* the squid. I tried to warn you back at the city – but you wouldn't listen."

"I didn't understand you then!"

"You Breathers don't try to understand – that's your whole problem!"

"I'm trying now. What is that monster? And who is the Professor?"

"I'll explain everything when we arrive."

"Arrive where?"

The seabed suddenly fell away. A steep valley sloped down, leading way, way deeper than the ocean ridge Aquora was built on. The swordfish dived. The water grew darker.

Far below, Max saw a faint yellow glimmer. As he watched it grew bigger and brighter, until it became a vast undersea city of golden-glinting rock rushing up towards them. There were towers, spires, domes, bridges, courtyards, squares, gardens. A city as big as Aquora, and far more beautiful, at the bottom of the sea.

Max gasped in amazement. The water was dark, but the city emitted a glow of its own

– a warm phosphorescent light that spilled
from the many windows. The rock sparkled.
Orange, pink and scarlet corals and seashells
decorated the walls in intricate patterns.

"This is – amazing!" he said.

Lia turned round and smiled at him. "It's our home," she said. "Sumara!"

Series 1: COLLECT THEM ALL!

An evil wizard has enchanted the magical beasts of Avantia. Only a true hero can free the beasts and save the land. Is Tom the hero Avantia has been waiting for?

FERNO
THE FIRE DRAGON
978 1 84616 183 5

SEPRON
THE SEA SERPENT
978 1 84616 482 8

ARCTA
THE MOUNTAIN GIANT
978 1 84616 484 2

TAGUS
THE HORSE MAN
978 1 84616 486 6

NANOOK
THE SNOW MONSTER
978 1 84616 485 9

EPOS
THE FLAME BIRD
978 1 84616 487 3

DON'T MISS THE
BRAND NEW SERIES OF:

Series 15: VELMAL'S REVENGE

WARDOK
THE SKY TERROR

978 1 40833 487 4

XERIK
THE BONE CRUNCHER

978 1 40833 489 8

978 1 40833 491 1

978 1 40833 493 5

COMING SOON